For Ron —T. S.
For Pen & Jake —S. L.

STERLING CHILDREN'S BOOKS
New York

An Imprint of Sterling Publishing Co., Inc.

STERLING CHILDREN'S BOOKS and the distinctive Sterling Children's Books logo
are registered trademarks of Sterling Publishing Co., Inc.

Text © 2021 Tammi Sauer
Cover and interior illustrations © 2021 Stephanie Laberis

ISBN 978-1-4549-4188-0

Distributed in Canada by Sterling Publishing Co., Inc.
c/o Canadian Manda Group, 664 Annette Street
Toronto, Ontario M6S 2C8, Canada
Distributed in the United Kingdom by GMC Distribution Services
Castle Place, 166 High Street, Lewes, East Sussex BN7 1XU, England
Distributed in Australia by NewSouth Books
University of New South Wales, Sydney, NSW 2052, Australia

For information about custom editions, special sales, and premium and corporate purchases,
please contact Sterling Special Sales at 800-805-5489 or specialsales@sterlingpublishing.com.

Manufactured in China

Lot #
2 4 6 8 10 9 7 5 3 1
09/21

sterlingpublishing.com

Cover and interior design by Jo Obarowski

Lovebird Lou

written by **Tammi Sauer**   illustrated by **Stephanie Laberis**

STERLING CHILDREN'S BOOKS
New York

"I love you."

Lou came from a long line of lovebirds.

"I love you more."

Lovebirds were all Lou knew . . .

"No, I love you more."

. . . until his flock visited the other side of the island.

The pelicans were great at figure eights.

The flamingos were wonders on the water.

The nightingales had the gift of song.

"Wow!" said Lou. "All those birds are amazing!"

Then something occurred to Lou.

"Lovebirds are so ordinary," said Lou. "I want to be a pelican!"

His mother pinched his cheek. "Okay, cupcake."

That morning, Lou flapped as hard as he could.

He swooped and looped across the sky.

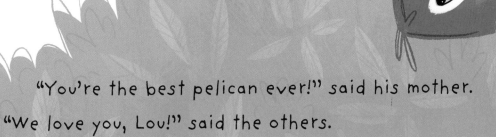

"You're the best pelican ever!" said his mother.

"We love you, Lou!" said the others.

All was well until . . .

The lovebirds scooped him right up.

"I think I'd rather be a flamingo," said Lou.

His father tweaked his beak. "Sure thing, sugar cookie."

That afternoon,

Lou stretched as tall as he could.

He waded into the water then balanced on one leg.

"I've never seen such a brilliant flamingo in my life!" said his father.

"We love you, Lou!" said the others.

All was well until . . .

Splash!

The lovebirds patted Lou dry.

"Perhaps I'd make a better nightingale," said Lou.

"Okie-dokie, artichokie," cooed his parents.

Before long, Lou tottered across a branch.

He cleared his throat.

He gave it everything he had.

"Screech. Screech. SQUAWWWWK!"
The lovebirds thought it was beautiful. "Bravo!"

The nightingales?
Not so much.

Lou stared at all the other birds and sighed.

He was not meant to be a pelican or a flamingo or a nightingale.

"Being a bird is for the birds," said Lou. "Maybe I'll just be a rock."

The lovebirds helped Lou find the perfect spot.

#1 ROCK

Lou sat.

And sat.

And sat.

He was an excellent rock.

That night . . .

"Wow," said Lou, "it's so dark out here."

A little while later . . .

"Whoa," said Lou, "it's so wet out here."

Roughly one minute after that . . .

"WAAAHHH!" cried Lou.

"IT'S SO SCARY OUT HERE!"

Lou did not need a pelican or a flamingo or a nightingale.

This situation called for one thing . . .

"We love you, Lou!" said the lovebirds.

"I love you, too!" said Lou.

Awwww . . .

The next day,

the pelicans flew in fancy formation.

The flamingos flocked in charming pairs.

The nightingales sang a brand new song. "La-la-la-la-love!"

And Lou?

He knew being a lovebird was, well, lovely.

Lovebirds were good at the most important thing of all.